# RUMPELSTILTSKIN

Afterword by:
Betty Jane Wagner
Chair, Humanities Division
National College of Education

Library of Congress Number: 79-27140

1 2 3 4 5 6 7 8 9 0 83 82 81 80

Printed and bound in the United States of America.

Library of Congress Cataloging in Publication Data

Daniels, Patricia.
  Rumpelstiltskin.

  (Raintree fairy tales)
  SUMMARY: A strange little man helps the Miller's
daughter spin straw into gold for the king on the
condition that she will give him her first-born child.
  [1. Fairy tales. 2. Folklore — Germany]
I. Nightingale, Sandy. II. Rumpelstiltskin.
III. Series.
PZ8.D188Ru    398.2'1'0943   [E]    79-27140
ISBN 0-8393-0252-5 lib. bdg.

# RUMPELSTILTSKIN

Retold by Patricia Daniels
Illustrated by Sandy Nightingale

**Raintree Childrens Books**
Milwaukee • Toronto • Melbourne • London

There was once a poor miller who had a beautiful daughter. He boasted to everyone he met of her beauty and cleverness, until even the king wished to meet her. When the king saw her, he agreed that she was indeed lovely.

"But what good is beauty alone?" the king asked the old miller. "What makes your daughter special?"

"She has a great talent," said the miller, eager to impress the king. "She can spin straw into gold."

The king was impressed, for he liked nothing better than gold. He took the girl to a far room in the palace. Its floor was covered thickly with straw.

"If what your father says is true, you will spin this straw to gold by morning," the king said. "If not, you will die." And he locked the girl into the room.

The poor girl had not the slightest idea of how to spin straw into gold. As she sat crying, a strange little man appeared in the room. He was very small, and his beard hung down to his knees. "Why do you cry?" he asked.

"I must spin this straw to gold," the

girl said, "and I don't know how."

The little man laughed. "What will you give me to do it for you?"

The girl gave him her necklace, and he sat down at the wheel. Soon the room was full of gold, and the man vanished just before the rising of the sun.

When morning came, the king was amazed to find that the miller had spoken the truth. His heart was filled with greed. He took the girl to a bigger room filled with even more straw.

"Spin this by morning," he said.

As soon as the girl was alone the little man appeared again. "What will you give me this time?" he asked.

The girl gave him her ring, and he sat down at the spinning wheel. Soon the room was filled with gold.

T he king was very happy to see so much
gold. He took the girl to a huge room. It
was filled with straw. "If you can spin
this, you will become my queen," he said.

The girl was crying when the little man
appeared. "I've nothing more to give you,"
she said.

"Give me your first child when you are queen!" said the man. The girl agreed. "Who knows what will happen before that?" she thought.

When the king saw the gold he married the miller's daughter. A year went by, and she had a beautiful baby.

The new queen had almost forgotten the little man, when one day he appeared in her room. "It is time to keep your promise!" he cried. The queen began to cry bitterly. The little man felt sorry for her.
"You have three days to guess my name,"

he said. "If you do, you may keep the child."

The queen's servants searched the kingdom for names. "Is your name Kasper, Melchior, Belshazzar?" she asked.

"No!" laughed the man. "You have two more days to guess."

On the next day the queen tried all the strange names she knew. "Is it Sheepshanks, Crookshanks, Spindleshanks?" she asked.

"No!" he shouted.

The queen's servants could find no more names. "But I did see an odd sight," said one.

"I saw a little man dancing around a fire
and singing,
   'Tomorrow I brew, today I bake,
   And then the child away I'll take,
   The lady cannot win the game,
   For Rumpelstiltskin is my name.' "
The queen was delighted.

When the little man came the next day,
the queen was ready.
     "Is your name Cherry-nose?"
she asked.
     "No!" laughed the man.
     "Is it Half-pint?"
     "No!" he cried and reached for the child.

"Is it, perhaps . . . Rumpelstiltskin?" said the queen.

"Some witch has told you that!" screamed the little man. In his rage, he stamped his foot, and it went right through the floor. Then he vanished, and never troubled the queen or the kingdom again.

With your finger follow the path the Queen must take to find Rumpel-stiltskin's name. Some clues from the story will help you on your way.

START

FINISH

(For the answer, turn to the last page.)

# The Story of Rumpelstiltskin

"Rumpelstiltskin", like all folk tales, was told for hundreds of years before it was ever written down. No one knows who first made it up, but someone who heard it retold it to someone younger and that person grew up and told it again. So the story lived even after the storyteller died.

About 175 years ago, two brothers, Jacob and Wilhelm Grimm, began collecting old German tales. They listened to an old woman of the village, Frau Katerina Viehmann, and others tell "Rumpelstiltskin" and wrote down their words. They published "Rumpelstiltskin" as part of a very important collection of German folk tales called *Household Tales*. There are many versions of this story. You might enjoy these:

- *Rumpelstiltskin* by the Brothers Grimm, illustrated by Jacqueline Ayer (Harcourt, Brace and World, Inc. 1967).
- "Tom Tit Tot", pp. 1—9, in *English Folk and Fairy Tales* by Joseph Jacobs (G. P. Putnam's Sons).
- "Rumpelstiltskin", in *About Wise Men and Simpletons, Twelve Tales from Grimm*, translated by Elizabeth Shub, etchings by Nonny Hogrogian (Macmillan Company 1971).
- *Rumpelstiltskin*, a story from the Brothers Grimm, illustrated by William Stobbs (Walck, Inc. 1971).

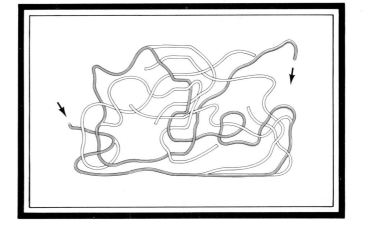